Put Beginning Readers on the Right Track with
ALL ABOARD READING™

The All Aboard Reading series is especially designed for beginning readers. Written by noted authors and illustrated in full color, these are books that children really want to read—books to excite their imagination, expand their interests, make them laugh, and support their feelings. With fiction and nonfiction stories that are high interest and curriculum-related, All Aboard Reading books offer something for every young reader. And with four different reading levels, the All Aboard Reading series lets you choose which books are most appropriate for your children and their growing abilities.

Picture Readers
Picture Readers have super-simple texts, with many nouns appearing as rebus pictures. At the end of each book are 24 flash cards—on one side is a rebus picture; on the other side is the written-out word.

Station Stop 1
Station Stop 1 books are best for children who have just begun to read. Simple words and big type make these early reading experiences more comfortable. Picture clues help children to figure out the words on the page. Lots of repetition throughout the text helps children to predict the next word or phrase—an essential step in developing word recognition.

Station Stop 2
Station Stop 2 books are written specifically for children who are reading with help. Short sentences make it easier for early readers to understand what they are reading. Simple plots and simple dialogue help children with reading comprehension.

Station Stop 3
Station Stop 3 books are perfect for children who are reading alone. With longer text and harder words, these books appeal to children who have mastered basic reading skills. More complex stories captivate children who are ready for more challenging books.

In addition to All Aboard Reading books, look for All Aboard Math Readers™ (fiction stories that teach math concepts children are learning in school) and All Aboard Science Readers™ (nonfiction books that explore the most fascinating science topics in age-appropriate language).

All Aboard for happy reading!

To my two beautiful monsters,
Lauren and Alexandra—B.B.

For Callie—B.H.

Text copyright © 2002 by Bonnie Bader. Illustrations copyright © 2002 by Bryan Hendrix.
All rights reserved. Published by Grosset & Dunlap, a division of Penguin Young Readers
Group, 345 Hudson Street, New York, NY, 10014. ALL ABOARD MATH READER and
GROSSET & DUNLAP are trademarks of Penguin Group (USA) Inc. Published simultaneously
in Canada. Printed in the U.S.A.

Library of Congress Cataloging-in-Publication Data

Bader, Bonnie, 1961–
　　100 monsters in my school / by Bonnie Bader ; illustrated by Bryan Hendrix.
　　　　p. cm. — (All aboard math reader. Station stop 2)
　　Summary: Jane Brain, the only non-monster at Frank N. Stein Elementary School, is
unhappy because she is the only student who didn't find 100 items to bring for show-and-
tell on the 100th day of school.
　　[1. Show-and-tell presentations—Fiction. 2. Monsters—Fiction. 3. Schools—Fiction.
4. Counting.] I. Title: One hundred monsters in my school. II. Hendrix, Bryan, ill.
III. Title. IV. Series.
PZ7.B1377　Aac　2002
[Fic]—dc21

　　　　　　　　　　　　　　　　　　　　　　　　　　　　2002007879

ISBN　0-448-42859-8 (pbk)　　　B　C　D　E　F　G　H　I　J

ISBN　0-448-42875-X (GB)　　　A　B　C　D　E　F　G　H　I　J

100 MONSTERS
IN MY SCHOOL

By Bonnie Bader
Illustrated by Bryan Hendrix

Grosset & Dunlap • New York

There are 100 monsters in my school.

There are 25 witches in my reading group.

They can fly through any book they read.

There are 25 ghosts in the lunchroom.

They love eating "scream cheese"

and jelly sandwiches.

There are 25 vampires in my gym class.

They can swing from the highest places.

There are 25 werewolves

in my music class.

My ears hurt when they sing.

Usually, I like school.

I like to read books.

I read slowly.

I like to eat lunch.

I eat peanut-butter-

and-jelly sandwiches.

I like gym class.

I can walk

on the balance beam.

I like music.

I sing very softly, but very high.

9

But the worst day of school

is the 100th day of school.

All the monsters in my school

love the 100th day of school.

I do not.

Our teacher, Ms. Vampira,

told us that we each have to bring

in 100 things for show-and-tell.

What should I bring in?

100 books? Too heavy.

100 thumbtacks? Too sharp.

"I want tomorrow to be spook-tacular!"

Ms. Vampira said.

All the monsters in my class were excited.

I was not.

"I do not want to go to school tomorrow,"
I told my mother at dinner.

"Why not?" she asked. "Are you sick?"
I shook my head no.

"I don't have anything to bring in for
the 100th day of school," I said.
My mom smiled.

"I'm not worried about you, Jane,"
she said.

"You will think of something.
Just use your head."

The next morning,

I walked to school slowly.

Wendy Witchman saw me

in the school yard.

She was dressed in all black,

as usual.

"What did you bring in for the

100th day of school?" she asked me.

I did not answer her.

"Well, I brought in

something very special.

But I'm not telling you what it is."

Wendy flashed me a smile

and flew away.

Sally Spookster was behind me in line.
"What did you bring in for the 100th day
of school?" she whispered.
I felt a chill run down my spine.

Sally was nice.

She was very, very quiet.

But she was nice.

"I did not know what to bring in,"

I told her.

"You will think of something, Jane,"

Sally told me.

We walked inside the classroom.

"Welcome to the 100th day of school!"

Ms. Vampira said.

"We will start our show-and-tell now,"

she said.

I slid down in my seat.

I did not want Ms. Vampira

to call on me.

I had nothing to show.

Or tell.

"Victor Fangly," Ms. Vampira said.

"Why don't you go first?"

Victor stood up and smiled.

All of his front teeth were missing.

Except for his two fangs.

They were very sharp and very pointy.

"I have brought in my fang collection,"
Victor said with a smile.

He held up a bunch of little bags.

"I have 10 cat fangs,
and 10 dog fangs," he began.

"I have 10 monkey fangs

and 10 alligator fangs.

I have 10 fangs from my grandma.

And 10 fangs from my grandpa.

They don't need their fangs anymore."

Everyone in the class laughed.

"I have 10 of my brother's baby fangs.

And 10 of my sister's baby fangs."

"I have 10 fangs
that I found
at the beach.

"And I have 10 fangs
that I'm going to leave
for the Fang Fairy."

At my house, the Tooth Fairy comes,

but I didn't want to say anything.

"That makes 100 fangs in all!" Victor said.

"Thank you, Victor!" Ms. Vampira said.

"That was fang-tastic!

Who will be next?" Ms. Vampira asked.

I slid down further in my seat.

"Pick me! Pick me!" Wally Wolfson called.

"Okay," Ms. Vampira said.

"I will show you 100 of my best howls,"
Wally said.

"Aooo!" Wally howled.

"That's 1."

"Aooo!" Wally howled even louder.

I put my hands over my ears.

It was a long way to 100 howls!

Ms. Vampira called on lots of other kids.

Sally Spookster told 100 spooky stories.

That took a long time.

And I got scared 100 times.

Bob Batty showed us his bat collection.

He had 50 fruit bats.

And he had 50 vampire bats.

That was a lot of bats.

I was glad they were in cages!

Wendy Witchman brought in
her cat collection.

"I have 20 cat stuffed animals,"
Wendy said.

She put the toys in front of
Ms. Vampira's desk.

"I have 20 cat keychains."

"I have 20 cat T-shirts.

I have 20 cat earrings.

That is really 10 pairs of earrings.

And I have 20 kitties."

Wendy opened up a big case.

20 little kittens came out

and looked at the class.

"Achoo!" I sneezed.

"Meow! Meow!" cried the cats.

I must have scared them.

The cats ran all over the room.

"My things!" Wendy cried.

"My 100 things!"

We raced around the room finding

all of Wendy's 100 things.

Finally, everything was found.

"Sorry," I told Wendy.

I handed her back the last kitty.

I tried not to sneeze.

Wendy took the kitty from me.

But she did not say a word.

Just then the lunch bell rang.

"Okay, class," Ms. Vampira said.

"We will finish our show-and-tell

after lunch."

Good.

That would give me some time to think.

I sat down at my lunch table.

But I did not feel like eating.

"Don't worry, Jane," Sally whispered.

"You'll think of something to show."

I put my head down on the table.

"Here," Sally said.

"These will make you feel better."

She handed me 5 marshmallow ghosts.

And 5 marshmallow mice.

Victor tried to cheer me up, too.

He gave me 5 bubble-gum bats.

And 5 bubble-gum owls.

Soon lots of kids at the lunch table had given me something.

I had 5
gummy worms.

And 5

gummy bears.

I had 5

licorice witches.

 And 5
licorice brooms.

I had 5
taffy pumpkins.

 And 5

taffy apples.

I had 5
cherry eyeballs.

 And 5

cherry lips.

 I had 5
vanilla stars.

And 5
vanilla moons.

 I had 5
lemon goblins.

And 5
lemon skeletons.

 I had 5
strawberry spiders.

And 5
strawberry snakes.

 And I had 5
chocolate cats.

And 5
chocolate rats.

I looked at all the things in front of me.

All 100 things!

Just then, Wendy walked over to the table.

"Yum!" she said. "Mind if I share?"

She reached down and popped

5 chocolate cats into her mouth.

Now I was left with only 95!

The bell rang.

It was time to go back to class.

"Let's finish our show-and-tell,"

Ms. Vampira said.

"Jane Brain," she said. "It is your turn."

Oh, no! What was I going to do?

I stood up.

But I tripped over my lunch bag

and fell down!

The class howled.

My face turned red.

"Settle down, class," Ms. Vampira said.

"Jane, are you okay?"

"Y-yes," I said.

"Why don't you take a minute and get
yourself together," Ms. Vampira told me.

"Glenda Specter, why don't you go next?"

I picked up my lunch bag

and peeked inside.

My mom had packed me a good lunch.

Too bad I didn't eat it.

I had a tuna sandwich.

I had an apple.

I had 5 chocolate cookies.

Wait! 5 cookies?

I was ready for show-and-tell.

"Thanks to my friends,

I have 100 treats

for the 100th day of school,"

I told the class.

"10 marshmallow treats.

10 bubble-gum treats.

10 gummy treats.

10 licorice treats.

10 taffy treats.

10 cherry treats.

10 vanilla treats.

10 lemon treats.

10 strawberry treats.

And 10 chocolate treats!"

I smiled at the class.

"And since there are 25 people in the class,

we each get 4 treats!" I said.

"Hurray!" the class shouted.

"I can't wait to sink my teeth into them!"

Ms. Vampira said.

The 100th day of school

didn't turn out so badly after all!